Cheer Up, Pig!

by Nancy Jewell

Pictures by Ben Shecter

Harper & Row, Publishers
New York, Evanston, San Francisco, London

To my dear friend Liz Birmingham Wellman

"I feel good," said Pig,
staring at a patch of sunlight on the barn floor.
"I'm so happy I can't wait to tell somebody!"
Pig ran outside.
"Where is everybody?" he called. "It's me, Pig!"
No one answered.
"Oh, well," said Pig, "I'm here anyway."
Then he had an awful thought.
Maybe everyone was hiding.

"This is silly.
I'm just feeling sorry for myself," he said.
"Feel happy again, Pig!"
Pig waved his curly tail.
"I said feel happy, Pig!" he shouted.
Pig rolled over in the mud.
Pig rolled over again.
"I love mud!" said Pig.
"So why does it feel so cold and awful?
I must be hungry."

Pig stuck his head in his trough.
"This food has no taste.
Maybe I'm not taking big enough bites."
Pig took bigger bites, smacking his lips.
"It's no use.
I don't feel like eating alone.
I don't feel like doing anything alone."

9

Pig heard happy shouts coming from the woods.
"Oh, no!" he cried.
"I bet all my friends are playing a game together,
and they forgot to ask me!
I'll go to sleep,
then I won't feel lonely."

Pig shut his eyes
and lay very still.
"Think of nothing, Pig," he said.
The wind rattled the branches of the maple tree.
A tractor cranked loudly.
"It's too noisy to sleep!"
Pig tried again.

13

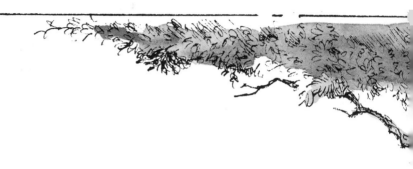

"Think of floating, Pig.
You are a feather.
You are a feather drifting along on the wind."
Pig sighed, almost asleep.
"Now you are drifting gently over the pond," he whispered.
Pig rolled over in his sleep.

"UGH!" he yelled, opening his eyes.
He was lying in a big puddle of water.
"You're not a feather, Pig,
you're just a pig."
Pig lay on the ground, too sad to get up.

"I know! I'll tell myself jokes.
Then I'll feel good again.
Knock, knock," said Pig.
"Who's there?" answered Pig.
But nobody was there.

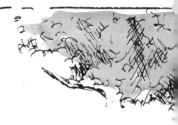

"I GIVE UP!" shouted Pig.
"How can I tell jokes by myself?"
Pig stared at the big maple tree.
"I wish I was a tree.
Trees never feel lonely."
Pig sighed.
"I am going to cry," he said.
"That is the one thing I can do by myself."

19

Pig lay down on his back.
He sniffed a little sniff.
Then he sniffed a big, loud sniff.
A bird chirped loudly overhead.
"It's so noisy," said Pig.
"I can't even hear myself cry!"
He looked up at the maple tree.

21

Mama Robin was perched beside her nest on a high-up branch.
Suddenly three little robins hopped out of the nest.
Mama Robin flew in a little circle around the branch and back.
The first little robin did the same thing.
So did the second little robin.
"Pig," whispered Pig,
"can you believe you are seeing three baby birds
getting their first flying lesson?"

23

The third little bird stood on the branch and didn't move.
"Come on, baby bird!" shouted Pig.
The little robin flapped its tiny wings.
Then it, too, flew once around the branch and back.
"I knew you could do it!" shouted Pig.

Pig did a little dance on his hind legs.
A silver dandelion puff floated by Pig, tickling his nose.
"I wonder where you're going,"
said Pig, chasing after the puff ball.
It floated right over his trough.
"Have a good trip, puff," called Pig, stopping to eat.
"Food, you don't taste half bad.
Hmmm!" Pig plunged his whole head into the trough.
Then he went over to his mud and rolled over.
"Mud, now you are beginning to feel nice and muddy."
"Pig!" someone called.
Pig didn't answer.
He wanted the someone to go away
so he could keep rolling in the mud.
"Pig!" someone shouted.
"Who's that?" said Pig crossly.
"It's me," said Duck.

"What are you doing, Pig?"
"Rolling in my mud."
"Aren't you lonely?" asked Duck.
"No," said Pig, standing up.
"How can you have fun all by yourself?" asked Duck.
"It's easy," said Pig.
"But since you are here,
I will tell you a joke."

"Say 'Knock, knock,' Duck."
"Knock, knock," said Duck.
"Who's there?" said Pig.
"I don't know," said Duck, looking around.
"*You* are, silly!" said Pig.
Duck and Pig laughed so hard
they both fell down in the mud.
"Ick," said Duck.
"I'm going to my pond to take a bath."
"I'll see you later," said Pig.
"I'm taking my bath in the mud."
Duck left.

"I'm glad I'm not a feather.
I'm a pig!" said Pig happily,
as he rolled over and over in the mud.